A SPEED BUMP & SLINGSHOT
MISADVENTURE

NIGHT OF THE LIVING WORMS

Dave Coverly

SQUARE
FISH

Christy Ottaviano Books

Henry Holt and Company ✶ New York

SQUARE
FISH

An imprint of Macmillan Publishing Group, LLC
175 Fifth Avenue
New York, NY 10010
mackids.com

Our books may be purchased in bulk for promotional, educational, or business use. Please
contact your local bookseller or the Macmillan Corporate and Premium Sales Department
at (800) 221-7945 ext. 5442 or by e-mail at MacmillanSpecialMarkets@macmillan.com.

Library of Congress Cataloging-in-Publication Data
Coverly, Dave, author, illustrator.
Night of the living worms : a Speed bump and Slingshot misadventure / Dave Coverly.
pages   cm
"Christy Ottaviano Books."
Summary: Jealous of his brother, Early Bird, who always gets the worm, Speed Bump
embarks on an adventure with his best friend Slingshot.
ISBN 978-1-250-09050-8 (paperback)   ISBN 978-1-62779-551-7 (ebook)
[1. Birds—Fiction. 2. Sibling rivalry—Fiction. 3. Brothers—Fiction. 4. Best friends—Fiction.
5. Friendship—Fiction. 6. Humorous stories.] I. Title.
PZ7.1.C684Ni 2015   [Fic]—dc23   2014043846

Originally published in the United States by Christy Ottaviano Books/
Henry Holt and Company
First Square Fish Edition: 2016
Square Fish logo designed by Filomena Tuosto

5 7 9 10 8 6 4

AR: 3.7 / LEXILE: 650L

For my parents, Carol and Lee, who always told us we could fly . . . until the day my sister, Cathy, took them literally, put on a Batman costume, and jumped face-first off the top of the slide.

Don't miss these other books by Dave Coverly:

Night of the Living Shadows

Dogs Are People, Too:
A Collection of Cartoons to Make Your Tail Wag

The Very Inappropriate Word,
written by Jim Tobin

Sue MacDonald Had a Book,
written by Jim Tobin

CONTENTS

CHAPTER ZERO

NOT-SO-SWEET DREAMS

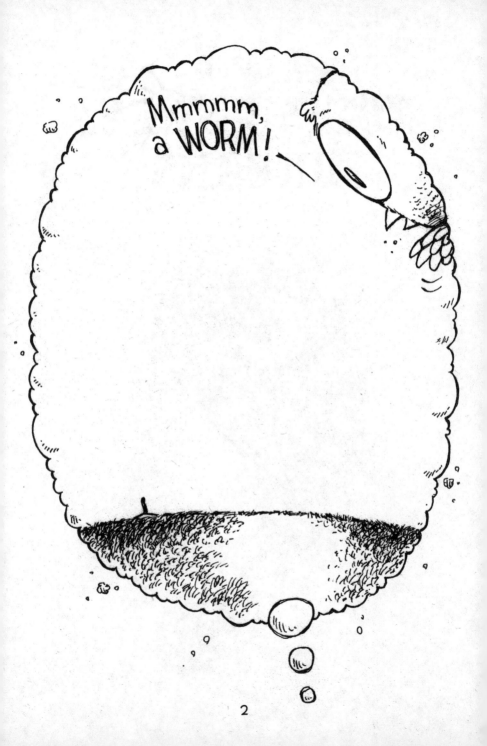

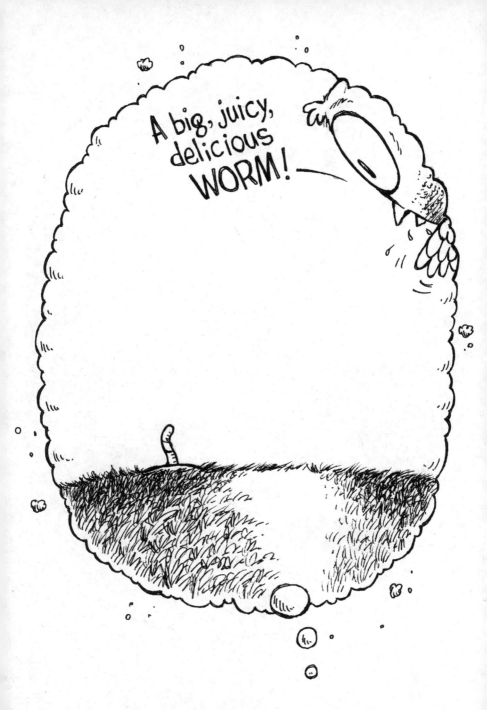

6

CHAPTER ONE

BIRDS OF A FEATHER

A little bird tweeting in the
window at the top of the large
Sycamore tree woke Speed Bump
from a restless sleep.

He took off the headphones he wore to bed every night (he *always* fell asleep listening to his favorite music), let out a loud yawn, scratched his tail feathers, and walked to the window.

His best friend, Slingshot, was already up, *slingshotting* berries at squirrels. The big rubber band he'd hooked around two tree branches made a loud *kaboing* sound every time he fired another berry.

KABOING!

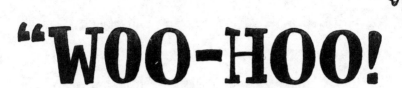

"WOO-HOO!

Did you see the look on that
squirrel's face? That berry
got him right in the *derrière*."

Speed Bump yawned. "In the *what*?" he asked, rubbing his sleepy eyes.

"*Derrière*. That's French for 'behind.'" Slingshot had started using French words after he got lost flying south last winter.

He had ended up in New Orleans,
where he met a French Hen he thought
was the most beautiful bird in the world.
Now he was practicing his French so he
could impress her next winter.

Slingshot put down the rubber band, winked at Speed Bump, and yelled to the squirrel, "Sorry, little buddy!"

He turned back to his friend. "You had that same nightmare again, didn't you?" "Yeah . . . Wait. How did you know?"

"A little bird told me—well, tweeted me. Plus you've got bad nest-head."

Speed Bump sighed and pulled some twigs from his head feathers. He hated that he flew so slowly. He hated that he had such a hard time waking up in the morning.

He hated that Early Bird always
got the worm before he could himself.
And the fact that Early Bird was his
brother . . . Well, that just made it even
worse.

"Speedy, you worry too much. Who cares if Early Bird always gets the worm?" Slingshot said. "There's a lot of other stuff we can eat. Berries and seeds and nuts and those delicious little crunchy bugs that wiggle in your mouth . . . Mmmm, delicious little crunchy bugs . . . How I love them."

Slingshot drooled a little bit,
and a familiar, faraway look came
over his eyes.

"Yeah, but he's not *your* brother,"
Speed Bump said. "And besides, seeds
and nuts are *boring*, and I don't *like*
those crunchy bugs. They're all dry
and sour, and those scratchy legs get
stuck in my throat. *Gack*."

"Scratchy legs . . . Mmmm. Hey, you know what my grandma says about you?"

"Your grandma says things about me?"

That Speedy Bump boy ought to get his chubby little bottom out of bed earlier instead of moping around all day!

Speed Bump rolled his eyes. He couldn't fly any faster.

His wings were tiny.

His tail feathers were short.

And his head, well, it was kind of large compared to the rest of his body.

He'd tried every way he could think of to get up earlier and beat his brother to the worm. But nothing ever worked.

First he'd stayed up all night, but by dawn he was so tired that he started hallucinating.

Then he'd asked Slingshot to wake him early, but he always slept right through the commotion.

One time he even drank coffee.

But that stuff only made him hyper,
and then he felt sick and needed to
lie down.

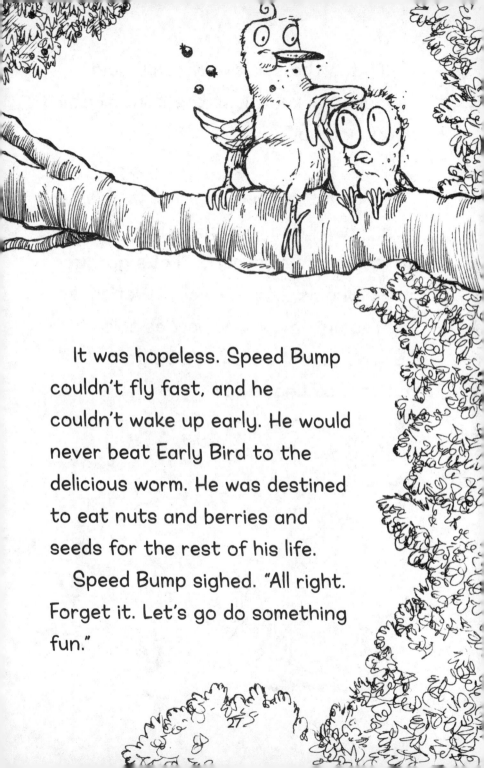

It was hopeless. Speed Bump couldn't fly fast, and he couldn't wake up early. He would never beat Early Bird to the delicious worm. He was destined to eat nuts and berries and seeds for the rest of his life.

Speed Bump sighed. "All right. Forget it. Let's go do something fun."

27

"That's the spirit, *mon ami!*" said Slingshot. "I know just the thing that'll cheer you up!"

"What?"

Slingshot popped a berry into his mouth and tried unsuccessfully to wipe off the berry mustache. "Let's go fly above people, and . . . well . . . let's just say I've eaten a lot of berries this morning, and I *really* need to go to the . . . you know, *GO!*"

"Do you mean what I think you mean?" Speed Bump asked.

"Oh yeah. TARGET PRACTICE!"

"All right! Dibs on the first one we see!" Speed Bump yelled.

32

CHAPTER TWO

BIRDS OF OTHER FEATHERS

Sweet child, I love you
more and more,
Though I'll always be
a trifle sore.

Speed Bump woke up late the next day to the sound of the Grackle in the home below screeching the same song she sang every morning. It was a tune from the old country about how much it hurt to lay a square egg. Elderly birds were so odd sometimes.

He took off his headphones,
stretched his wings, and . . .

"Sorry, little bro, didn't mean to scare you," said Early Bird. "I brought you the last bite of the worm I got this morning."

He squeezed the piece of worm. "There's still a little juice left, I think."

Speed Bump stared at the worm. He wanted it more than anything. But he just couldn't take it. He'd promised himself a long time ago that he wouldn't eat that worm until he'd earned it.

Not that he ever *would* earn it.
Speed Bump and Early Bird might have
been born at the same time, but they
couldn't have been more different.
Speed Bump had been so sleepy that
his mom had to knock on his shell to
wake him up and tell him it was time to
break out of his egg.

Early Bird, on the other hand, had been so strong and energetic that he taught himself to fly . . . *before he even hatched.*

"So?" Early Bird dangled the end of the worm. "You gonna try it for once?"

Speed Bump sighed. "Nah," he said. "I promised I'd look for seeds and stuff with Slingshot."

"More for me, then!" Early Bird threw
the piece of worm in the air, then
swallowed it in one gulp.

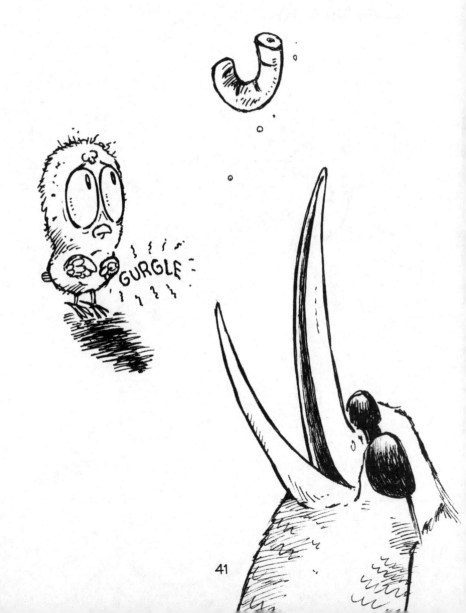

"Guess I'll catch ya later, unless you catch me first! HA-HA! Maybe someday!" He was gone before Speed Bump's stomach could finish rumbling.

Slingshot poked his head in the window.

"Wow, you look tired enough to molt. Another nightmare?"

"Nah, it was that ol' Grackle singing. But my brother was just here, tempting me with a worm. I didn't want it. Not really. I guess not."

"Aw, c'mon, let's go *manger.*"
Slingshot bobbed and weaved his way
to the ground.

Speed Bump fell like a stone from his
window, wildly flapping his tiny wings to
soften his plunge. He knew *manger*
meant "to eat" in French, because that
was Slingshot's favorite thing to do.

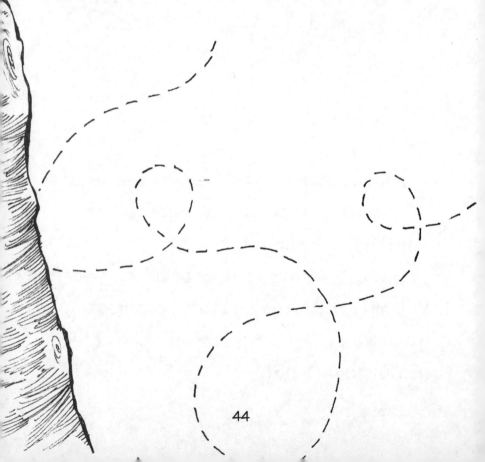

44

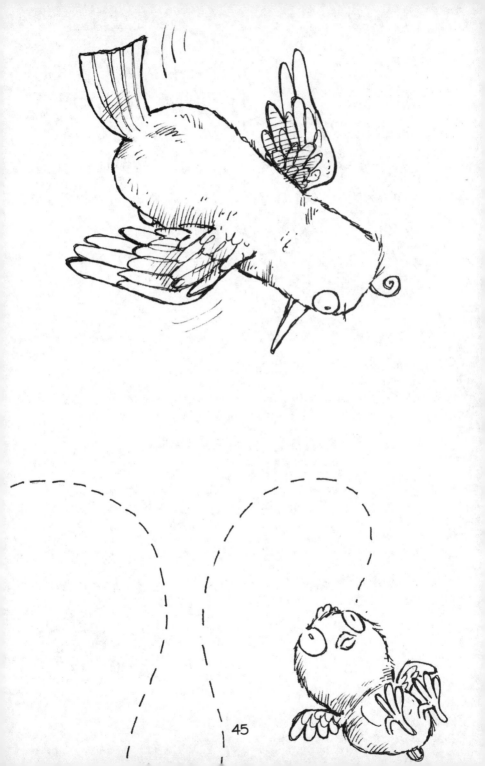

45

squawked the Parrots. (They were on
vacation from the jungle, visiting the
Belted Kingfisher.)

said the
Canada
Goose.

cackled the Mockingbirds.

swooned the Lovebirds.

said the Dodo.

On and on it went all day, just like it did every day. Finally, with the sun glowing behind the pine trees, and their bellies full of nuts and berries and seeds (and, in Slingshot's case, a couple of mysterious things that he ate even though neither of them knew what they were), the friends went their separate ways home.

That night, with the birds' words flying around in his head, Speed Bump had a harder time falling asleep than usual. He tried classical music, like Birdthoven's Fifth Symphony. He tried jazz music and put on some Birdie Holliday. He even tried pop music and listened to Lady CawCaw. None of it could settle him down or block out the cruel voices of those Mockingbirds.

You're not as fast as he is!

Speed Bump's mother had always told him, "Never, ever, *ever* leave your nest in the middle of the night. The darkness is full of shadowy beasts that will eat you, and others that will squeeze you until you POP."

Then her face would get even more serious. "And there are rumors of a giant bird with giant eyes and giant claws and a beak as sharp as a RAZOR! No, no, no, never go out at night."

Of course, Speed Bump decided to
leave his nest anyway. He knew it was
definitely a bad idea, but he was all out
of good ones.

CHAPTER THREE
THE WORMS ARE REVOLTING!

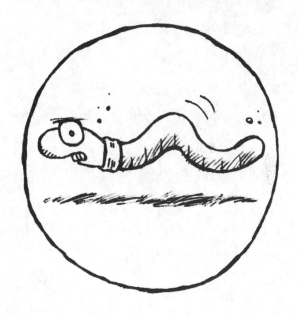

"You know, food isn't the only thing I think about—oh, YUM!" Slingshot snatched a firefly out of the air. His beak glowed as he munched it down. "I always wanted to try one of those. Kind of hot 'n' spicy. Let's find more."

They walked and walked. Slingshot
ate all kinds of flying bugs and spiders
still sticky with webbing, while Speed
Bump nervously hummed his favorite
songs.

A couple of raccoons startled them,
laughing and rolling a garbage can as
they crossed their path and ran out
of sight.

Slingshot saw the pair of large
glowing circles first.

LOOK! Those must
be the biggest
fireflies EVER!

Uh, Slingshot, I
don't think those
are fireflies....

No, they DEFINITELY weren't fireflies. They were a pair of giant eyeballs on a pointy-eared head with a razor-sharp beak that was coming straight at THEM! The beak opened wide. Speed Bump jumped into Slingshot's arms, and they both screamed like hungry baby birds waiting for their mommies.

WHOOSH!

The massive flying beast
swooped past. There was a
snapping sound.

Then it flew back into
the night sky, carrying a
stealthy snake that had
been sneaking up behind
Speed Bump and Slingshot.

The bird winked one of its giant glowing eyes at them and disappeared into the darkness.

There was a scuttling noise under a bush. "Man, I . . . **BUUUUURRRRP** . . . I HATE those things!" A mouse peered out at them. "**BUUUUURRRP** . . . Hey, what can I say? I burp when I'm nervous."

Then the mouse was gone, its burps getting fainter as it scurried away.

Maybe my mom was right. Maybe the nighttime IS too dangerous.

Too dangerous and too WEIRD.

Uh-huh. Let's go home.

Uh, sure...but *mon ami*?

Yeah?

Which way is home?

"We're lost?" Speed Bump screamed and jumped into Slingshot's arms again.

"Stop DOING that! C'mon. Let's try this direction."

The buddies walked...

and walked and walked and walked. They were surrounded by strange, unfamiliar sounds...

and the high-pitched echo of a distant *burp*

They tried flying. It was so dark, though, that they kept bumping into trees. After the fourth crash, they decided to walk again.

The ground in front of them *was* moving back and forth. Shadowy figures had risen from the dirt and were swaying eerily in the moonlight.

WORMS!!

Speed Bump had never seen so many. It seemed as if there were hundreds, maybe thousands, maybe millions, popping out of the earth. They were all so BIG and FAT!

A little whiskered snout poked out
from the bushes once again.

Just as Speed Bump was wondering how mean a worm could really be, a tall shadow rose up over the Nightcrawlers. It seemed like the biggest, creepiest worm in the history of all slimy things. The other Nightcrawlers snapped up straight, except for a couple of smaller ones that dove back into the ground to hide.

"The big one is talking to them!" Slingshot whispered. "What's it saying?"

"How should I know?" the mouse squeaked. "Do I look like I speak Wormese?" Then, with one last BURP, it was gone in the dark underbrush.

Speed Bump edged closer. He was nervous, curious, and suddenly very hungry. Nightcrawlers were scary, but they also smelled delicious. He glanced at Slingshot, who was standing in a puddle of drool.

Then the towering Nightcrawler let out a horrible, wicked laugh.

That was when Speed Bump saw something terrible silhouetted in the moonlight. The thing looked like an enormous worm, but it wobbled as if it was made of rubber, and its arms were actually sharp metal hooks.

The rest of the Nightcrawlers began chanting, and not in Wormese.

GET EARLY BIRD!
GET EARLY BIRD!
GET EARLY BIRD!

"Oh no, Slingshot!" Speed Bump squeaked. He knew this could mean only one thing. "The worms are out to get Early Bird! We can't let him eat that . . . that THING! It has hooks! Sharp, pointy hooks! My brother's so fast he won't even know it's dangerous until it's too late!"

Speed Bump felt dizzy. His brother might drive him nuts, but he was still his brother, and the thought of him eating the fishing worm was . . .

Well, it was just too awful to even think about.

Family Trip to Gull Lake, '08

CHAPTER FOUR

HATCHING A PLAN

& OTHER BAD PUNS

No one had ever woken up Early Bird. It was a Very Serious Rule among all the animals:

Early Bird Sleeping
DO NOT DISTURB!

Because if he didn't get enough sleep, he would be tired, and if he was too tired, he might snooze past dawn, and if he snoozed past dawn, he wouldn't get the worm.

And if Early Bird didn't get the worm, who knew what other unexpected and crazy things might happen in the world?

BOW TO ME, BIRDS!

No, it would all be too unpredictable.
Early Bird *had* to get the worm. That
was just the way things were.

"You're right. It's against the Very
Serious Rule," Speed Bump said,
practically reading Slingshot's mind.
"We need to stop the Nightcrawlers
ourselves."

They hatched plans, but got
eggsasperated because they knew
none of them would work, and this was
no *yolking* matter. All their ideas to
stop the Nightcrawlers were as terrible
as their puns.

"Let's face it,"
Speed Bump groaned.
"We're just a couple
of birdbrains."

"If only I had my slingshot," mumbled
Slingshot. "We could knock 'em out with
nuts and berries."

"SLINGSHOT!"

Speed Bump yelled.

"Who, me?"
"Not you! Your
slingshot! You're a
genius, Slingshot!"

"Who, me?"

"Yes, you! I'll explain later. First we need to get home!"

"Home?" The voice was right behind them. A pair of giant glowing eyes blinked twice. Speed Bump screamed and jumped into Slingshot's arms once again.

I thought you boys looked a little lost.
You live in the large Sycamore, am I right?
How did he KNOW?
Whoa... owls really ARE wise!

There was a tiny burp in the bushes.
The owl's head spun all the way around.

That sounded like a MOUSE burp!

Hey, don't owls EAT mice?

RUN, LITTLE MOUSY! RUN!

"Soda Pop!" the owl said.

Speed Bump and Slingshot looked at each other. "Soda Pop?" they repeated at the same time.

"Yep. But you can call me just Soda, or just Pop. It's all good," Soda Pop said as he climbed onto the owl's back. "Are we going on a trip, Hoover? Can I go with you guys?"

"Waaait a minute," Speed Bump said. "Don't owls make you nervous?"

"Not *this* owl. Snakes make me
nervous. And Nightcrawlers. And cats.
And clowns, but that's another story."

At the mention of Nightcrawlers,
Speed Bump remembered Early Bird.
"Hey, we need to go! NOW!"

Hoover turned his head back toward
them. "What's the big rush, boys?"

Meanwhile, Slingshot was trying, unsuccessfully, to make his head spin all the way around.

Speed Bump caught his breath and quickly told Hoover about Early Bird and the Nightcrawlers and the horrible, rubbery worm with the hooks and his own plan to save his brother.

Hoover spread his giant wings. "Sounds like you boys need help with a plan that big!" He turned his head around again to talk to the mouse. "Whaddaya say, Soda Pop? Shall we?"

Soda Pop just nodded. And burped.

"Man, night animals are definitely weird. And the big one has serious snake breath," Slingshot whispered. But they both had to admit that they got home a lot faster flying in Hoover's tailwind.

CHAPTER FIVE

IS IT TOO LATE FOR EARLY BIRD?

A thin ray of light was just starting to show on top of the tree line as Speed Bump tightened his oversize headphones and stepped in front of the slingshot. Hoover, Soda Pop, and Slingshot pulled back the large rubber band as far as it would go, as Speed Bump leaned into it. A couple of squirrels watched from the end of a branch, twitching their tails and chattering in Squirrelese.

✱ "I think the birds have gone crazy."
✱✱ "They've ALWAYS been crazy."

"Wait . . . wait . . . not yet . . ." Speed Bump said as they all stared at the hole in the oak tree where Early Bird slept.

Just then, a blurry figure shot out of the hole and streaked past them. Early Bird was off to get the worm!

"FIRE!" Slingshot shouted. And with a loud grunt, they let go of the rubber band, then dove out of the way when it snapped back with a big

KABOING!

With the force of the launch, Speed Bump zipped through the morning sky, his tiny wings flapping uncontrollably and his headphones threatening to fly off his head. He whizzed past Early Bird with such speed that he never saw the surprised look on his brother's face.

The wind whistled around Speed Bump's beak, and before he could catch his breath to scream, he was diving right at the wormhole.

The evil-looking rubber worm was already there, dangerously sticking up from the ground, its sharp hooks waiting for Early Bird to swoop in. Instead, Speed Bump slammed into it with a thud. The hooks stuck to his headphones as he bounced and tumbled across the dirt with the rubber worm whipping along beside him.

At that moment, the king of the Nightcrawlers popped out of the same wormhole to enjoy its victory over Early Bird—

and that was exactly when Early Bird zoomed in for his breakfast.

By this time, the Robins and the
Swallows and the Wrens and all
the others had gathered around,
shouting. . . .

"Actually," said Early Bird, "what I got appears to be a Nightcrawler. And my brave brother got the . . . the . . . well, I don't know *what* that scary-looking thing is," Early Bird said. "But holy crow, am I glad Speed Bump stopped me from getting it first!"

Early Bird flipped the *real* Nightcrawler over to Speed Bump. "Here, little bro. I think this is yours. You definitely earned it!"

The birds started cheering and
squawking and whistling and tweeting.
Some of the squirrels went a little
crazy, even the ones with berry juice
splattered on their *derrières*. Soda Pop
was so excited he burped the whole
alphabet, and Hoover's head spun
around four times.

Speed Bump caught the Nightcrawler
in his beak and stared at it for a second.
Yes, he thought. *I DID earn a worm!
Finally, a worm is MINE! IT'S ALL MINE!*
He imagined the gooey, delicious
Nightcrawler sliding down his throat
and into his growling stomach.

He closed his eyes, and, for the first
time in his life, Speed Bump ate a worm.

But then . . . his eyes got big, his knees went weak, and his beak turned the color of pea soup.

So off they flew. Speed Bump was sure he'd be the *rotten egg*, but it was okay. He'd saved his brother, he'd made some new friends, and he'd finally tasted a worm. It was a good day.

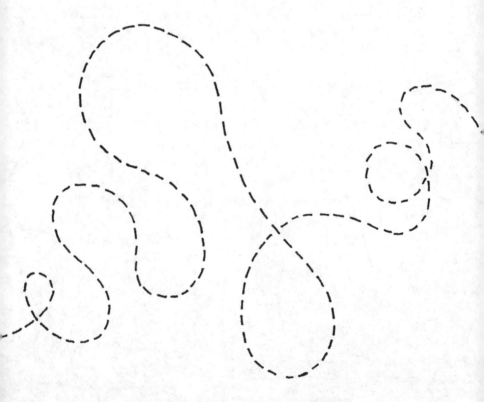

And besides, Speed Bump knew his best buddy, Slingshot, would always be waiting for him, no matter how long it took him to get there.

GOFISH

DAVE COVERLY

In addition to being a writer/ illustrator of books for kids, you are also a syndicated cartoonist with your own panel, *Speed Bump*. Did your panel influence the characters in The Misadventures of Speed Bump and Slingshot? How so?

Yes! My syndicated cartoon influenced this book on a bunch of different levels, actually. For starters, I drew Speed Bump and Slingshot in the same style I would draw birds in my panel—and then I made them just a little goofier. But it was important that I draw them in a style that I found comfortable, because I knew I was going to be drawing them over and over (and over and over for new books about them!). Also, when I draw my syndicated panels, I try to think of jokes that come out of situations, as well as some puns. For these misadventures, I really did the same thing, which is put the bird buddies in situations and then see if I could make something kind of funny happen. Sometimes it felt like I was writing and drawing a whole bunch of bird cartoons, but they were all connected by a story.

How is creating cartoons different from writing and illustrating novels? Are there any similarities?

It's different in one important way: When I write and illustrate a cartoon panel, I have to tell the ENTIRE story in that one little box. But when I write and illustrate a novel, I know I have a plot and I'm aiming toward a conclusion. I need the characters to act silly, but I also need to them to act in a way that will get them to that conclusion. It's almost like I have a movie in my head. So when I create a novel, I try to draw all the details of the movie. But when I do a panel, I only draw the one scene from the movie that will best tell the story.

Are you an Early Bird or a Night Owl?

I am the nightest of Night Owls ever. Mornings, ugh! Not even a gummy worm would get me out of bed. I love staying up late when everyone else is asleep and the house is super quiet—it's a great time to draw birds. And evil worms.

What did you want to be when you grew up?

I knew in third grade that I wanted to be a cartoonist! Maybe because I loved to draw and use my imagination, and because being an adult seemed so weirdly complicated.

What's your most embarrassing childhood memory?

Oh, great, now I have to relive this. . . . When I was in seventh grade, I was the lead in a school play, and halfway through the most important scene, I totally forgot my lines. And it was the night the whole school and the parents were watching.

What's your favorite childhood memory?

When I was in sixth grade, my dog, Tigger, got off his leash and ran away. I thought he was just chasing a squirrel or exploring, but he didn't come back that day. Or the next day. Or the next! I remember being in school and being so sad that I couldn't even concentrate. On the fourth day that he was gone, I got off the bus to walk home, and as I came around the corner, I saw him in our garage, barking at me as I ran toward him. That has to be one of my happiest memories.

As a young person, who did you look up to most?

Definitely my parents. They didn't *tell* me how to act, they showed me, and they were wise enough to make sure I was paying attention. Even now, when a complicated situation comes up, I ask myself: What would my parents do? And if I'm still confused, I just call them. Because they're still around and they have a phone.

What was your favorite thing about school?

Doodling in the margins of my notebook.

Did you play sports as a kid?

I tried all kinds of sports! First baseball and football, and a little bit of soccer, but then I discovered tennis and fell in love with it. I played all the way through high school, and even got a scholarship to play in college. It's a great sport, because you can play it your entire life.

Where do you write your books?

I write my books in two different places, depending on what time it is. If it's late at night, I love to write in my studio, because it's in the attic of my house and it's very quiet and private. But if I write during the day, I LOVE to go outside and write on my porch. I live in a neighborhood where the houses are very old and close together, so while I'm writing I get to see the world going by and still feel like I'm a part of it.

What challenges do you face in the writing process, and how do you overcome them?

Writing can be very frustrating—you probably already know that! For me, it's very important that I have peace and quiet, so I can get lost in the world of the characters. But since I work at home, sometimes I get interrupted by my dog barking, or by one of my kids asking me a question. Or I'll just get distracted because I'm hungry and the kitchen is right downstairs. So I set goals for myself about how much I have to do before I allow myself to take breaks.

What is your favorite word?

Foible. It sounds funny, and it also describes cartoons perfectly.

If you could live in any fictional world, what would it be?

Wait—this world isn't fictional?

Who is your favorite fictional character?

I love Gollum from The Lord of the Rings. He's so complicated—sometimes you love him and sometimes you don't like him at all.

What was your favorite book when you were a kid? Do you have a favorite book now?

I have so many favorite books now! When I was really young, I read *The King, the Mice and the Cheese* over and over. When I got just a little bit older, I read all of The Hardy Boys books, and Encyclopedia Brown. I really liked mysteries—and I think Speed

Bump and Slingshot might find themselves in a mystery of their own soon. . . .

What advice do you wish someone had given you when you were younger?
BUY STOCK IN APPLE COMPUTERS.

What would you do if you ever stopped writing?
Sleep.

If you were a superhero, what would your superpower be?
Flying. Like a bird. And then, like a bird, I might go to the bathroom on top of the houses of people I don't like. That's a superpower, right?

Do you have any strange or funny habits? Did you when you were a kid?
Okay, here's a crazy one that hardly anyone knows about me: Ever since seventh grade, I've always put my right shoe on first. ALWAYS. I'm not kidding. It would drive me crazy now to put my left shoe on first. I started it on a whim, and now it's forty years later and I'm still doing it. I don't even know why.

What would your readers be most surprised to learn about you?
I can shoot lasers out of my eyes. I just choose not to.

Speed Bump and Slingshot are on a quest
to rise in the ranks from Bird Scouts to Eagle
Scouts. But when yet another misadventure
goes wrong, they both end up trapped in the
mall! Will they survive the night, or ever figure
out how to escape?

READ ON FOR A SNEAK PEEK!

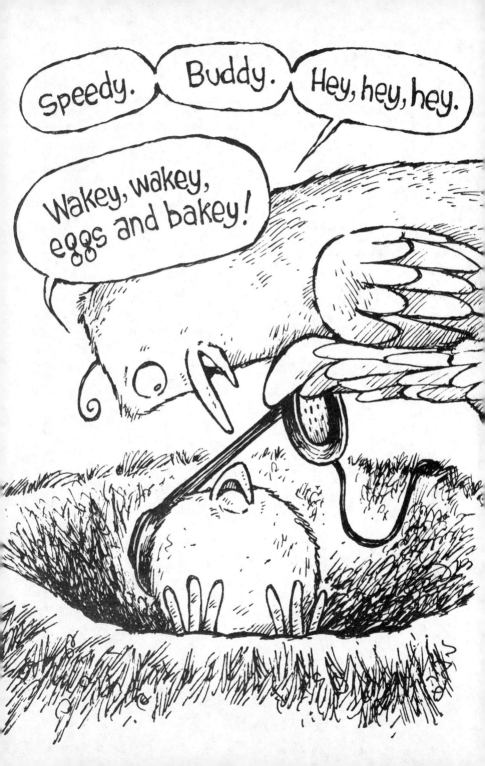

After his daring adventure rescuing his brother, Early Bird, from the evil Nightcrawlers, Speed Bump had been so exhausted that he fell asleep while flying.

Luckily for him, he'd been right over a forest of soft Yellowwood trees and didn't even wake up when he landed. Slingshot put his buddy on his back and flew him all the way home.

Speed Bump hadn't even so much as twitched when Slingshot dropped him into his nest, stuck the headphones over his ears, and turned on Birdthoven's Symphony no. 7 in Beak-Flat Major.

But now that Speed Bump was awake, Slingshot had more important things on his mind.

"Aren't you STARVING? I can hardly go 48 MINUTES without eating!" Slingshot groaned.

"Not really. I still sort of have that nasty Nightcrawler taste in my mouth."

"Mmmm, Nightcrawlers . . . Well, I HAD to get you up. Today's the scavenger hunt, remember?"

Speed Bump and Slingshot were members of the Bird Scouts. It was their favorite club, and it was where the two of them had met when they were little, before their fuzzy baby feathers had even developed into flight feathers. They'd done all their activities together and earned all their Bird Badges except for one: the Scavenger Badge.

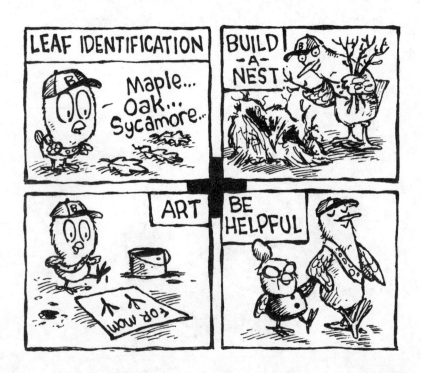